CANADA

Newfoundland
and Labrador

Prince
Edward
Island

Quebec

Nova
Scotia

Ontario

New Brunswick

Canada All Year

Per-Henrik Gürth

Kids Can Press

Ready, set, let's explore Canada!

January

Race along the Rideau Canal!

May
Tiptoe among the tulips.

June

Catch a festival of fireworks.
Ooh! Ahh!

August

Pick a sweet harvest of blueberries — yum!

October
Watch the Pacific salmon run.

November

See the prize-winning pigs
at the Royal Winter Fair. Oink!

December

Go dogsledding through the snow
in Nunavut — mush!

Home sweet home!

What an adventure! Let's do it again!

For Nasrin Sinjari-Gürth

Kids Can Press acknowledges the financial support of the Government of Ontario, through the Ontario Media Development Corporation's Ontario Book Initiative; the Ontario Arts Council; the Canada Council for the Arts; and the Government of Canada, through the BPIDP, for our publishing activity.

Published in Canada by
Kids Can Press Ltd.
25 Dockside Drive
Toronto, ON M5A 0B5

Published in the U.S. by
Kids Can Press Ltd.
2250 Military Road
Tonawanda, NY 14150

www.kidscanpress.com

The artwork in this book was rendered in Adobe Photoshop.
The text is set in Providence-Sans Bold and Good Dog Plain.

Written and edited by Yvette Ghione
Designed by Rachel Di Salle

This book is smyth sewn casebound.

Manufactured in Tseung Kwan O, NT Hong Kong, China, in 3/2011 by Paramount Printing Co. Ltd.

CM 11 0 9 8 7 6 5 4 3 2 1

Library and Archives Canada Cataloguing in Publication

Gürth, Per-Henrik
        Canada all year / Per-Henrik Gürth.
ISBN 978-1-55453-709-9

1. Canada — Pictorial works — Juvenile literature. 2. Seasons — Canada — Juvenile literature. 3. Months — Juvenile literature.
I. Title.

FC58.G87 2011   j971   C2011-900089-X

Kids Can Press is a *Corus*™ Entertainment company